Written and illustrated by Katie

Chapter 1

Goldilocks, as we all know, was a curious girl. She was a very foolish girl too, and as we remember from her incident with the three bears, her curiosity sometimes landed her in trouble.

What had she been thinking that day? Entering a stranger's house, eating their food, breaking their belongings then falling asleep in one of their beds!

When Goldilocks returned home that evening she was so frightened, she had burst into tears and told her mother everything, and unsurprisingly, her mother had given her such a telling off.

Her mother was furious, she thought she had taught her daughter to behave better. But Goldilocks was a curious girl and no amount of teaching could remove *that* from her personality.

One morning as she sat for breakfast (in her own house, I should mention), Postman Paul knocked cheerfully on the door.

Goldilocks' mother went to the door and was given the usual bills, a leaflet about the health benefits of green tea from the Wicked Witch and a large letter stamped from the 'Courts of F.T.M.B.'. This stood for 'Fairy Tales and Make Believe' which I'm sure, you already knew.

"Oh my goodness!" her mother gasped; she was scanning the letter as she made her way back into the kitchen. Her eyes darted across the page as she read.

"What's wrong, mother?" Goldilocks asked. The ends of her golden curls were dipping in her cereal bowl and getting drenched in milk.

"You're being taken to court! The Bears are taking you to court! I thought we were past all of this!"

Her mother was in such a panic,
but Goldilocks, quite honestly, had
no idea what that meant.

"So...is that a *bad* thing?"
Goldilocks asked.

"Of course it's a bad thing!" her mother cried. "You could get sent to jail, or we might have to pay them money as compensation! We don't have any money, Goldi, we don't have enough to pay The Bears. And you can't go to jail! You'll make friends with criminals and get covered in tattoos, then you'll be released and bears everywhere will be too terrified to leave their homes!" her mothers eyes filled with tears as she spoke.

"Oh dear," Goldilocks muttered, then her eyes brightened as she spotted her reflection on the back of her spoon. "I'm sure I'll be fine! Look at me! As soon as I go to that court place, they'll see how pretty I am and let me go home." Goldilocks showed her very best, sweetest smile as her hair dripped all over the table.

Her mother smiled weakly, "Yes...I don't think that's how it works dear. Right, let's sort you a new dress."

Chapter 2

The day of the court case was fast approaching, Goldilocks was out (far away from The Bears' cottage, I might add) collecting blackberries from the bushes that swarmed in a small area of forest, just behind her house.

"Hello, Goldilocks," said a voice. It was Little Red Riding Hood (but today was Tuesday, so she was wearing her yellow hood).

"Oh, hi Riding Hood. I suppose you've heard about me going to court," Goldilocks muttered, scuffing the dry mud beneath her shoes.

"Yes, my father told me. It's such a shame, but it is the best way to get things settled.

My grandma took the Big, Bad Wolf to court after everything was over. She got so much compensation! After all, she was swallowed whole. And now, she has a restraining order against him, which means he can't come anywhere near her or our family...most importantly her bed."

Goldilocks worried.
"But we haven't got any money to pay The Bears and I already know not to go anywhere *near* their house again!"

"Wasn't there a thing about you breaking Baby Bear's chair?" Riding Hood asked.

"Yes...but I didn't know it wouldn't hold me! I'm not *that* heavy! He must be a *very* small bear if it could hold his weight and not mine." Goldilocks felt very insulted that the chair had collapsed.

As if I'm heavier than a bear. She thought crossing her arms.

"Well, why don't you get Mr Chopper to make him a new chair. A brand new, beautiful wooden chair. I mean, it is his job! That's why we called him to Grandma's house, we knew he'd be chopping wood somewhere and we knew he'd have an axe on him, the perfect tool to scare away a Big Bad Wolf wouldn't you say?" Riding Hood winked.

The idea was genius!
Goldilocks dropped all of her blackberries.

"Thank you!" she cried as she raced home to tell her mother.
Her mother was thrilled with the plan. She just wasn't sure how she would make an apple and blackberry crumble...without any blackberries.

The next morning (the day before court) Goldilocks and her mother invited Mr Chopper round for some breakfast.

Mr Chopper's first name was Alan. Alan Chopper. He had been a wood chopper since the age of nine when his father first began teaching him the trade. He had also won the 'Best Beard' competition for the last four years in a row.

Not many others can grow a beard like Alan.

"So, what were you thinking then?"
Alan enquired as he glugged his tea.

"Well, it needs to be special, *really* special.
Maybe you could carve something into it,"
Goldilocks' mother began.
"Or write his name on it!" Goldilocks
added.

"Right," said Alan as he stroked his wiry,
ginger beard. "I think I could sort that for
you."

"And please bring it with you to court."
her mother added with a smile.

The day finally arrived. Goldilocks' mother was rushing about like a headless chicken, faffing around and feeling flustered.

"Do we have everything?" she asked, "Yes, mother," Goldilocks replied, admiring herself in the mirror. "Do you have your apology letter?"

"Yes mother."
"Does Alan have the chair?"
"YES mother...can we go *now?"*
Goldilocks had been practicing her very best sweetest smile all morning and now, she was ready to leave and defend herself.

Chapter 3

A large crowd of people holding cameras and notepads were gathered on the steps outside the court house.

"Just ignore them dear, they're from the press. We don't want to be in any newspapers, so say nothing." her mother said sternly, pulling her closer.

They spotted Goldilocks and swarmed around her like a flock of vultures closing in on their prey. Goldilocks smiled nervously as the cameras flashed in her eyes.

"Miss Locks! Miss Locks!" they cried out from every direction.

Secretly, Goldilocks was enjoying the attention, she felt like a celebrity.

One reporter got right up to Goldilocks and shoved his microphone under her nose.

"Miss Locks - did you go into that house? Did you break their things? How are you going to win this case, Miss Locks?"
"I'm going to smile sweetly, that should work." Goldilocks replied.

"Goldilocks will tell the truth!" her mother hissed. "Now get that microphone out of her face before I throw it and *you,* into the river!" her mother pulled forcefully at Goldilocks' arm and quickly ushered her into the courtroom, her eyes remaining fixed on the reporter's terrified face.

The courtroom was ENORMOUS - the biggest room Goldilocks had ever seen! It made her mother feel even more anxious.
"Who are they?" Goldilocks asked, pointing to a mixed group of people and creatures who were sitting beside the judge.

"They are the jury members; they are the ones who will decide if you are guilty or not. So make sure you smile at them...*a lot!*" her mother whispered, fixing her dress.

Goldilocks began smiling immediately!

The judge sat high above everyone else so he could see the entire room. He was sitting on a pile of very large and heavy books to make him appear taller.

Everyone stood up and waited until they were told to be seated.

Goldilocks recognised him; he was one of the elves that lived in the bottom apartment in a block of flats on the other side of the forest. He had a large, white, wispy beard, icy blue eyes and small, half-moon glasses that perched on the end of his nose. He furrowed his brow as he looked across the room.

He adjusted his glasses and lifted some paperwork up towards his face,

"Miss Locks, you are here today as you have been accused of breaking and entering a private property belonging to The Bears family; of causing great distress to the family, willfully damaging furniture and eating food that was *not* for you. Do you understand the reasons for why you are here?" his voice was deep and *very* slow - he sounded as though he was about to fall asleep. He peered over his papers to look across at Goldilocks. The whole room was looking at her.

"Err…yes," she smiled nervously. "You may all be seated," the judge announced to the room.

Whilst two smart creatures (all dressed in black with funny wigs on) were talking about what had happened, Goldilocks looked around the room. All of a sudden, she spotted the three bears!

She hadn't seen them in a *long* time, but they still looked cross with her. She smiled sweetly, of course, but it didn't seem to work.

Mr Bear had a knobbly, wooden walking stick and was wearing a smart tie patterned with tiny porridge bowls. Mrs Bear was wearing a very fancy hat, and Baby Bear had his fur brushed down neatly and was wearing a little black bow tie. Looking at him closely, she really couldn't understand how that chair broke with *her* weight and not his!

"He must have weakened it." she muttered to herself.

The two smart creatures, (who were all dressed in black with funny wigs on), were called 'lawyers'. The Bears had a lawyer, and Goldilocks had one too. The Bears' lawyer was starting first. He was a fox named Francis, he was a sly looking fellow, (naturally) he was wearing a long black cloak with his fluffy orange tail sticking out the bottom, and his whiskers flickered as he spoke.

Goldilocks' lawyer was a Pixie named Perrin. He wore a tiny shimmery green suit under his cloak and his wings glistened as the sun, from the windows, shone through them.

Each lawyer had to fight the other (with words of course) and prove who was right.

So, Francis wanted to prove that Goldilocks was guilty, and Perrin wanted to prove that Goldilocks had simply made an innocent mistake, and The Bears should have kept their house locked up more securely. He seemed to think it was a good argument.

"I understand this was a *very* distressing day for you and your family, Mr Bear. Your home was broken into, food was stolen, items were damaged and you found a complete stranger in your bed!" Francis drawled.

"That's not true! I only slept in Baby Bear's bed!" Goldilocks stood and shouted. The judge banged his gavel and her mother pulled her back into her seat.

"Please, Miss Locks, I will sort this," Perrin whispered as he flittered above her head.

"It was a VERY bad day!" growled Mr Bear, looking straight at Goldilocks. She felt her cheeks burning red as she slunk down in her chair so he couldn't see her.

"My poor Baby Bear has been so upset. It was his favourite chair. And Mrs Bear hasn't made any porridge since! It just hurts too much."

Goldilocks looked over to Mrs Bear, who gently patted her eyes with a handkerchief that just so happened to match her hat.

It was then time for Perrin to call his first witness: the witch who live next door to Goldilocks and her mother.

"Mrs Witch-" Perrin began.
"Oh please, call me Mrs Snothubble dear, that's my real name," Mrs Snothubble smiled wide with just her four teeth showing, as a stringy piece of snot dangled from her nose.

"Tissue?" Perrin asked through gritted teeth, handing one over quite quickly before he vomited all over the judge.

Goldilocks remembered when she met Mrs Snothubble for the first time, (although she was allowed to call her Winnifred).

At first, Goldilocks was terrified of her! Her face, the colour of green sludge found at the bottom of a pond, warts stuck out in every direction, and her matted and mangled silver hair with an old, black crow nesting atop it.

Not to mention the snot - she seemed to have a never ending ball of it stuffed up her nose!

But Mrs Snothubble was a lovely witch and she often made 'bubble jam' for Goldilocks and her mother. It was a black cherry jam, and when you spread it on your toast it began to bubble! Hot bubbles of cherry jam would rise into the air which you'd pop with your tongue. And you'd have a delicious zingy taste burst into your mouth.

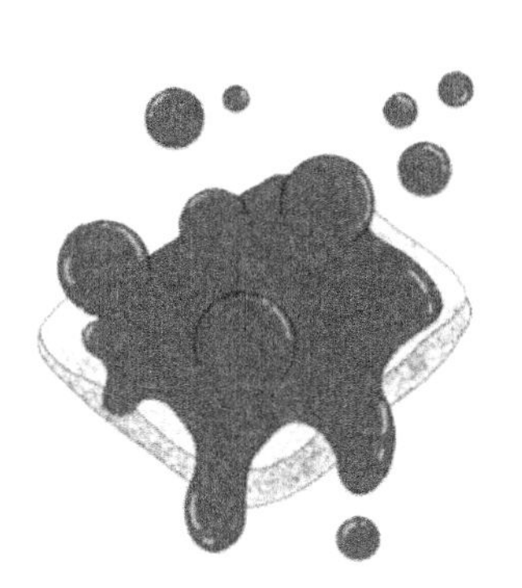

However, you'd have to catch the bubbles pretty fast because if they popped against anything else…well, safe to say there'd be a big, black jam splat that was *incredibly* hard to clean off, as Goldilocks' mother had discovered one morning.

She also had a cat called Flea. For the simple fact that he was covered in them, but he didn't seem to mind and they made excellent special ingredients in many of Mrs Snothubble's potions.

"Where were you on the day in question Mrs Snothubble?" asked Perrin.

"On what day, dear?" replied Mrs Snothubble, a wash of confusion came over her face.

"The day with The Bears."

"A BEAR! Oh goodness me!" Mrs Snothubble jumped from the seat screaming, and whistled for her broom to escape immediately.

"No! No, Mrs Snothubble, please stay calm. I'm talking about the day when Goldilocks went to The Bears' house," Perrin caught hold of the broom as it flew in from an open window on the roof.

"Oh of course, it was a Sunday dear," said Mrs Snothubble.
"Yes...we know that, but where were *you* on that day?" Perrin sighed.
"On what day dear?"

In truth, Mrs Snothubble was an incredibly talented witch that made delicious bubble jam...but her memory wasn't the best.

"Let's move on shall we?" Perrin smiled awkwardly as he handed over her broomstick, he couldn't help but feel he hadn't achieved much in helping Goldilocks' case.

"I've had a wonderful day," smiled Mrs Snothubble. She shuffled her way back to her seat and turned to the lady who sat beside her.

"What time is the bus coming dear?"

Chapter 4

The day seemed to go on and on and on! Perrin and Francis kept shouting at one another.

"The Bears left their home wide open for intruders, and who can resist the sweet smell of delicious warm porridge?" Perrin argued.

"This girl was only thinking of herself! She entered that house to cause nothing but trouble!" Francis argued back.

"The Bears never should have left their home; I believe they left the porridge as a trap. They knew someone would enter their home, and they wanted to catch them. Perhaps even to eat them! We know how unpredictable bears can be - luckily Goldilocks screamed for her life, or who knows what would have happened to her!"

"Goldilocks entered that house simply to intrude! Her own mother said in a statement that Goldilocks has never even liked porridge!"

It went back and forth, on and on like a very long and very *boring* game of tennis...but no one seemed to be winning.

Some members of the jury had even fallen asleep!

Then Francis called in another witness, Mr Oaks, the gigantic oak tree who stood behind The Bears' cottage in their back garden.

He had been uprooted to attend the court. He had to be airlifted in by a helicopter! He was standing in a wheelbarrow and a badger stood beside him, showering him every now and then with water from a watering can. The windows on the roof had to be opened so all his bushy branches could spread out.

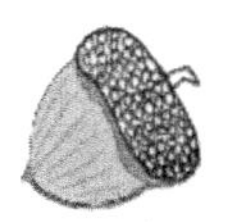 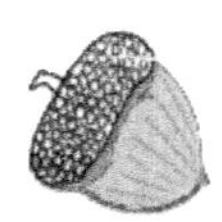 

"I saw her go in," Mr Oaks began, "and I saw her break Baby Bears chair. And I saw her through the bedroom window when she went upstairs to sleep. She looked so peaceful, but I should have woken her up! I've felt so guilty ever since, I'm The Bears' garden tree...and I let them down."

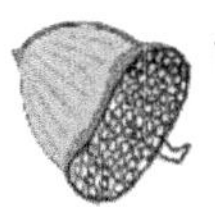 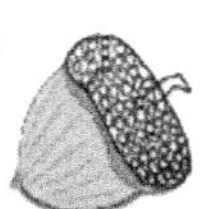

He suddenly burst out crying, but instead of tears - he cried acorns! They made an awful pinging sound as they bounced against the edges of the wheelbarrow.

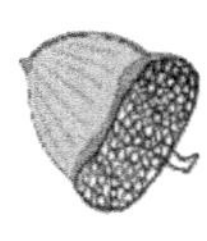

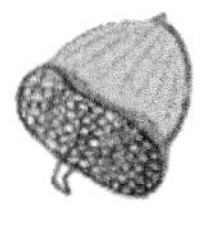

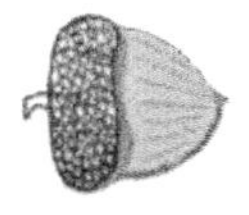

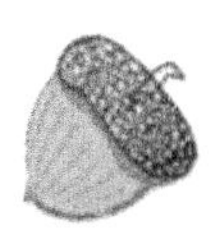

Suddenly, a scurry of squirrels ran into the court, climbing in through the windows and sneaking under the doors! They bustled about collecting up the falling acorns. Some of the squirrels even tried to bury them in the courtroom, one squirrel tried to bury an acorn in Mrs Bears' handbag! The squirrels fought and squabbled with each other trying to get the best ones.

Mr Oaks felt so embarrassed, he began to cry more! The squirrels scurried up and down his trunk, catching the acorns as they fell. Some acorns were even flung into the jury box. It was like a game of 'whack a mole' as one member of the jury jumped up, another sat down.

The squirrels scrambled around between their legs, under their arms, and all over them just to get at the acorns. There were screams and shouts, Mr Oaks was blubbering away, the badger was trying to whack the squirrels away with the watering can...then:

Bang!
Bang!
Bang!

The judge banged his gavel and it echoed around the entire room, and silence returned to the court. The squirrels grabbed what they could and ran out of the room.

"May I ask you Mr Oaks, don't you face the forest when standing in The Bears garden? So why were you facing the house?" Perrin asked.

"Well, I do face the forest but, sometimes in the morning, the sun shines right onto The Bears' cottage, and I do love to feel that warm sunshine on my leaves, so, I turn myself around…and that's when I saw *her!*"

One of Mr Oaks' long branches stretched out and pointed right at Goldilocks- the little twigs on the end almost poked her in the eye!

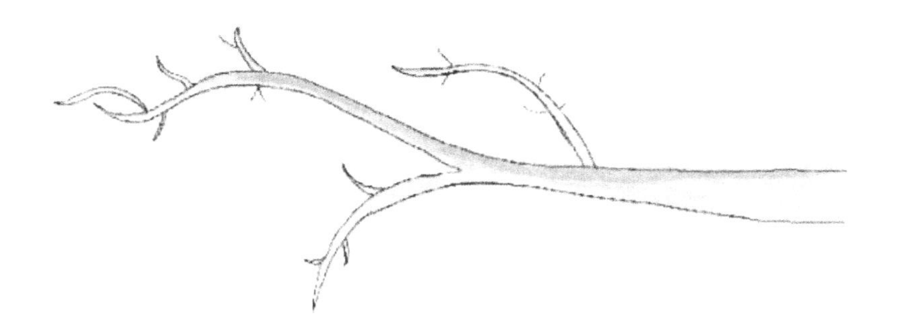

"But how do we know that? Where is the proof? I think, Mr Oaks, you heard about the story of Goldilocks and you didn't want The Bears to think you'd let them down by missing it all, so you lied about seeing her. You didn't see her at all, you were facing the other way. You just want to get this poor girl into trouble! She may have gone into The Bears' house, but you, Mr Oaks did NOT see what happened."

Perrin flew right over the jury to make his point loud and clear.
Some of them began nodding their heads and jotting down notes.

"No! I did see her, I did!" The tree began to cry again. And before you could say, 'it's raining acorns', all the squabbling squirrels were back and the mad affair was happening all over again!

Goldilocks felt a bit sorry for Mr Oaks, but only a little bit; he was on The Bears side after all.

The court was calmed again and Mr Oaks was removed and taken back to The Bears' cottage. He was feeling quite overwhelmed.

Chapter 5

"I call Goldilocks to the stand!"

Francis finally said, and everyone in the room gasped. It was the moment Goldilocks had been waiting for. She felt her little legs begin to wobble beneath her, her cheeks burning red as everyone's eyes were watching her. Her throat felt dry, her mouth felt numb. She didn't know whether to run away or cry. Her whole body began to shake and her apology letter quivered in her hands.

Goldilocks tried her hardest to smile as sweetly as she could, but her cheeks wobbled like jelly on a plate.

"Miss Locks, how well do you know The Bears family?" Francis questioned. He began pacing up and down the room swishing his tail slowly from side to side.

Goldilocks looked confused, "well, I don't really know them at all." she replied.
"Oh, so do you usually enter the homes of people you don't know?" Francis hissed, smirking at the jury.

Goldilocks gave a little giggle as she remembered an incident from a few years ago, "Actually, there was the time when I was visiting my grandma and she lived at number thirty one but I thought she said number *forty one*. So I went into number *forty one* where a family of pigs were having a mud bath, but that was a genuine mistake...oh, but so was The Bears' house, that was a mistake too!" Goldilocks explained, smiling at the jury.

"No, Miss Locks. You went for a walk that morning. That beautiful, Sunday morning and you smelt the sweet smell of Mrs Bears' porridge. You looked into the cottage, saw no one was home and took a chance! I don't think you even sat on Baby Bears' chair - I think you smashed it! You ate that porridge, realised it was wrong, and so you wanted it to look like a robbery, to cover your tracks. Like a thief had burst into the house, ate their food, smashed their belongings and then ran away. But you were so tired after smashing Baby Bears' chair that you went upstairs and foolishly fell asleep, and you were caught in the act! Nothing like your grandmas's house. No mistake at all. Now isn't that true?"

Francis' voice was so loud and so scary. He flicked his tail behind him as he turned away.

Goldilocks could feel the tears well up in her eyes.

"No," her voice was almost a whisper, so shaky and quiet. She could barely get her words out.

"No I didn't mean to," Goldilocks swallowed hard and raised her voice for all the court to hear, "it was a mistake, it was all an accident. Can I read my letter to The Bears please?" she asked, looking over at the judge.

"You honestly think The Bears want to listen to a letter!?" Francis blurted. "They don't want to hear a letter! They want their porridge back! They want their chair back that's what they want!" he banged his fist against the jurors table.

The judge removed his glasses and cleaned them on his cloak. "You may read your letter Miss Locks. But please know, it may make no difference to your case." he replied.

Goldilocks nodded and cleared her throat, "Dear The Bears," Goldilocks began, "please may I start by saying that I am a very sweet girl-"

"HA!" Mr Bear roared, his sarcastic laugh echoed around the room.
"Mr Bear, please control yourself. Do continue Miss Locks," the judge announced.

"I'd then like to add that sometimes I do silly things that get me into trouble. But I am completely harmless. I'm just a bit... silly."

Goldilocks then began explaining to the court a number of 'silly things' she had done in the past.

Like the time she began climbing a beanstalk from Jack's meadow as a dare, and not even getting a quarter of the way up before getting stuck.

The whole fire brigade had to come out and rescue her! It took them over three hours and three fire engines to get her back down.

Then another time when her mother had asked Goldilocks to water the flowers and trim the bushes. But Goldilocks got muddled up and ended up watering the bushes and trimming all the flowers. She wasn't sure how to 'trim' a flower, so she simply cut all their petals off, just leaving their stalks. Her mother cried for two days.

Then another time (quite recent actually), when she lost her lollipop. She spent most of the afternoon looking for it.

When she got into bed that night, she found it stuck in her hair. Her mother had to cut it out, then cut the rest of her hair to match. Goldilocks was more disappointed that her lollipop had to be thrown in the bin.

Goldilocks felt quite embarrassed sharing these stories with the court, but the jury had a good laugh.

"I'd like to address you now, if I may."

Goldilocks took a deep breath and turned to face The Bears. "Mrs Bear, my mum was right in her statement, I have never liked porridge, but your porridge was the *best* porridge I've ever tasted! It was so sweet, warm and delicious…I think you should make your own porridge packets and sell them for everyone to enjoy!"

Mrs Bear tried to hide her smile, but she felt simply giddy with delight. Mr Bear and Baby Bear never said anything about her porridge. Mr Bear would just complain about how hot it was.

"Mr Bear, I think the reason you have that walking stick is because your back is sore…and I think I know why. Your chair and bed were terribly uncomfortable, as hard as lying on a brick wall! I suggest you buy some more cushions and a softer mattress, and that will sort your back out."

Mr Bear sniffed the air thinking Goldilocks may be right. Mrs Bear raised an eyebrow at him. "Something I've been saying for years." she muttered under her breath.

"And Baby Bear: I'm so sorry for breaking your chair, I still don't know how I did it. I mean, you're a bear, you're obviously heavier than me, I can't weigh more than *you,* I'm taller than you but I'm not heavier. Like I say, you're a *bear,* a little bear but still a heavier bear than me-"

"Ahem!" her mother coughed loudly to stop her mid rant.

"Oh…yes, I'm sorry. I didn't mean to break it, and to show how sorry I am, we have had a special chair made just for you." Goldilocks smiled.

At that moment, Alan chopped his way through the courtroom doors!
"THEY DO OPEN, YOU KNOW!" the judge shrieked as splinters of wood scattered like an explosion.
Alan slid his axe back into the holder on his belt, and carried in the most exquisite chair anyone had ever seen.

The wood had been varnished all over, that it glistened in the sunlight. It was carved so beautifully, with toy planes, teddy bears and porridge bowls. And the words 'Baby Bear' were carved across the top.

Baby Bear squealed with excitement:
"I love it! I love it!"
Mrs Bear was almost in tears again.
"Did you make this just for him?" she asked Goldilocks.

"Well I didn't, but we asked Mr Chopper. I wanted to show you how sorry I was, I wanted to replace what I had broken. I am *really* sorry." Goldilocks replied, looking down at the floor.

Red Riding Hood nudged an old wizard sitting beside her, "that was my idea," she winked.

Mrs Bear turned to look at Mr Bear, he nodded his head and rose from his seat.

"This court case is over," he declared, raising his furry arms in the air. "We accept Goldilocks' apology and we certainly accept this new chair. We have sorted this amongst ourselves and we don't need the jury anymore."

Goldilocks gasped and rushed back to her seat. She hugged her mother tightly as her mother sobbed with joy. The whole courtroom cheered.

"Let's go home!" he added.

The jury looked very pleased, in fact almost everyone was pleased. Even Perrin and Francis had a cuddle!

But the judge was not pleased. "I should be working in a *very* special workshop today making toys! I took the day off to come here. For goodness sake!" he snapped, he slowly climbed down off of his pile of books (then climbed down a step ladder to reach the ground). Then he left the courtroom in quite a huff.

Chapter 6

A few weeks later, Mrs Bear was in the process of opening her own porridge factory. She decided to call it 'Just Right Porridge'.
Everyone around the forest was helping to get it ready, including Goldilocks.

It even reached the front page of *The Magic Mirror* newspaper!

Goldilocks and Baby Bear had great fun playing together, and she often had tea at their house - invited of course.

Mr Bear had taken Goldilocks' advice (even though his wife had told him many times before) and bought himself a softer bed and a more comfortable chair.

Within a month, he didn't need to use his walking stick anymore and he was sleeping much better too!
This was unfortunate for Mrs Bear, as he spent most of the night snoring. Snoring as loud as a…well, you know.

Goldilocks tried her best to curb her curiosity and tried to keep herself out of trouble as best as she could.

She came down for breakfast one morning when there was a knock on the door. "Hello Postman Paul," smiled Goldilocks as she opened the door and was handed a letter.

"Looks like you're going again," he tutted, the letter was stamped from the Courts of the F.T.M.B'!

Goldilocks slowly closed the door and cuatiously opened the letter. What had she done this time!? Who had she upset?

She scanned the letter as she returned to the kitchen,
"What's that for now!?" her mother cried.

"Mother...*you're* being taken to court..." Goldilocks muttered.
"WHAT!?" her mother shrieked.

"For...threatening behaviour towards a reporter. Apparently you said you'd throw him into a river?"

Her mother's jaw dropped and she turned white as a sheet.

"Right, let's sort you a new dress,"
Goldilocks smiled.

All books by Katie Budge can be found
on www.amazon.co.uk

Facebook: @ktbudgebooks
Instagram: kt_budge_books

Printed in Great Britain
by Amazon